CLUES AT THE CARNIVAL

By Ivy S. Ip
Illustrated by Duendes del Sur

Hello Reader — Level 1

If you purchased this book without a cover, you should be aware that this book is stolen property. It was reported as "unsold and destroyed" to the publisher, and neither the author nor the publisher has received any payment for this "stripped book."

No part of this publication may be reproduced in whole or in part, or stored in a retrieval system, or transmitted in any form or by any means, electronic, mechanical, photocopying, recording, or otherwise, without written permission of the publisher. For information regarding permission, write to Scholastic Inc., Attention: Permissions Department, 555 Broadway, New York, NY 10012.

ISBN 0-439-20232-9

Copyright © 2001 by Hanna-Barbera.
CARTOON NETWORK and logo are trademarks of Cartoon Network © 2001.
SCOOBY-DOO and all related characters and elements are trademarks of Hanna-Barbera.
All rights reserved. Published by Scholastic Inc.
SCHOLASTIC, HELLO READER, and associated logos are trademarks and/or registered trademarks of Scholastic Inc.

12 11 10 9 8 7 6 5 4 3 2 1   1 2 3 4 5 6/0

Designed by Maria Stasavage

Printed in the U.S.A.

First Scholastic printing, January 2001

SCHOLASTIC INC.
New York   Toronto   London   Auckland   Sydney
Mexico City   New Delhi   Hong Kong

, , , , and

were at the carnival.

They wanted to see the and

his in the magic show.

and the gang went to the

magic show .

"There is no magic show today," the  said.

"My magic 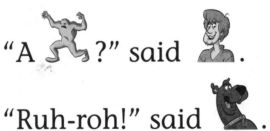 is missing!"

The pointed to some .

"A took my !" the said.

said.

"A ?" said .

"Ruh-roh!" said .

"We will find your ," said . ", , and I will follow the .  and  will look for clues."

"But,"  said, "we might run into the ."

"Rikes!" said .

 and  were afraid.

"Look, Scoob," said 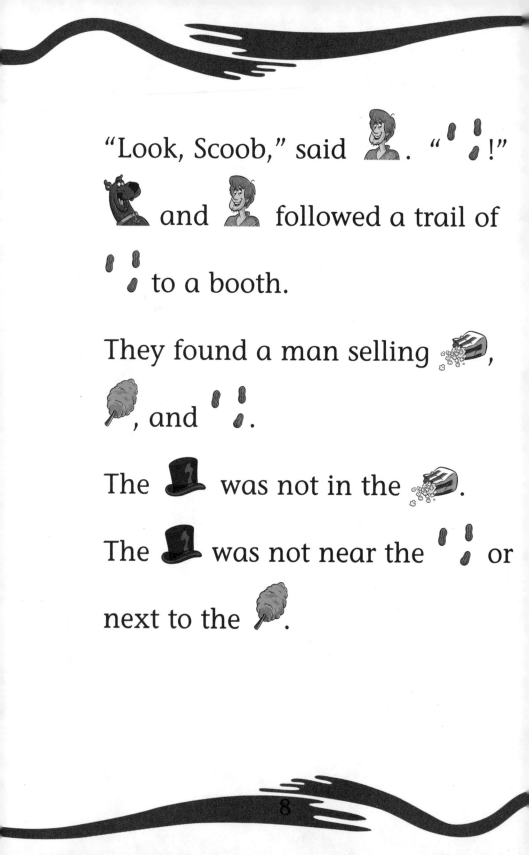. " 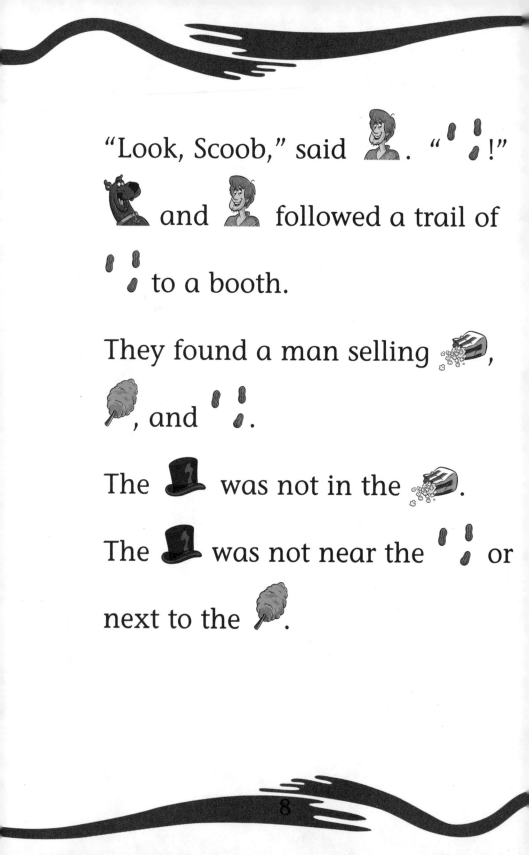 !"

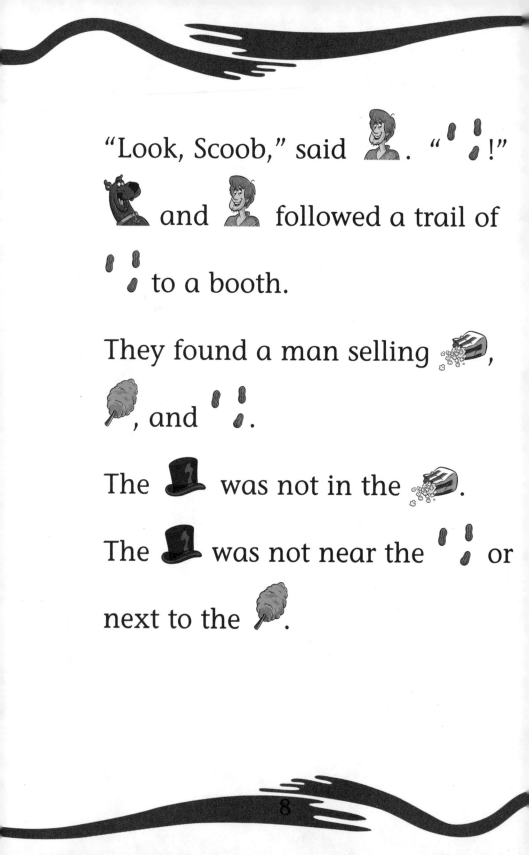 and followed a trail of

 to a booth.

They found a man selling ,

, and .

The was not in the .

The was not near the or

next to the .

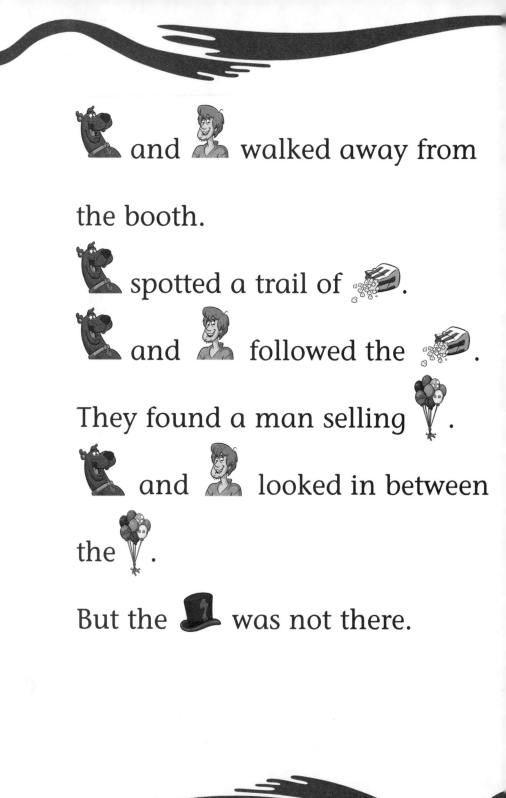

and walked away from

the booth.

spotted a trail of .

and followed the .

They found a man selling .

and looked in between

the .

But the was not there.

, and  followed

the  to a game booth.

Maybe the  was inside the

booth.

 looked inside a . He saw

a .

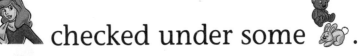 checked under some .

 looked above the .

But they did not find the or

the .

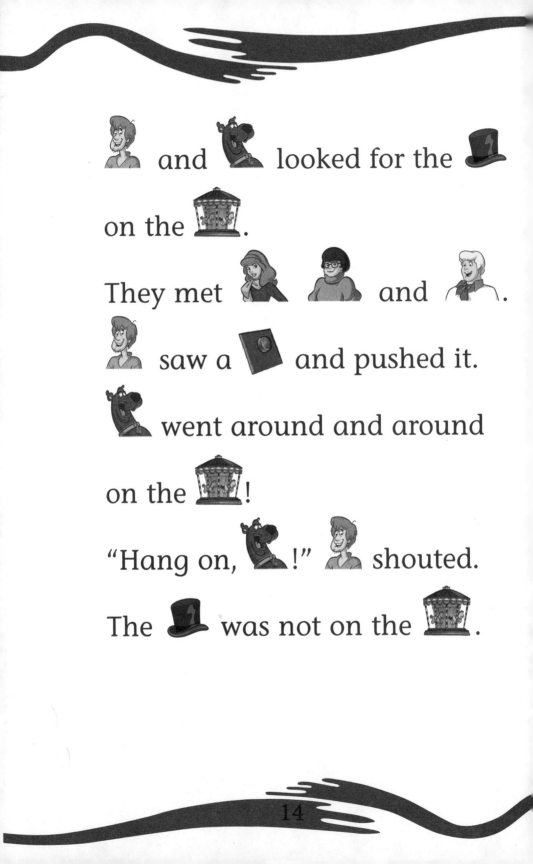 and 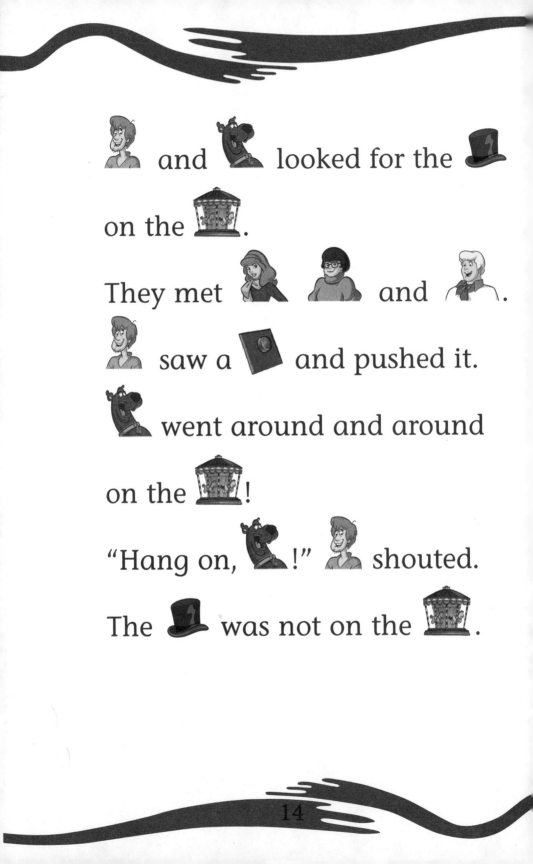 looked for the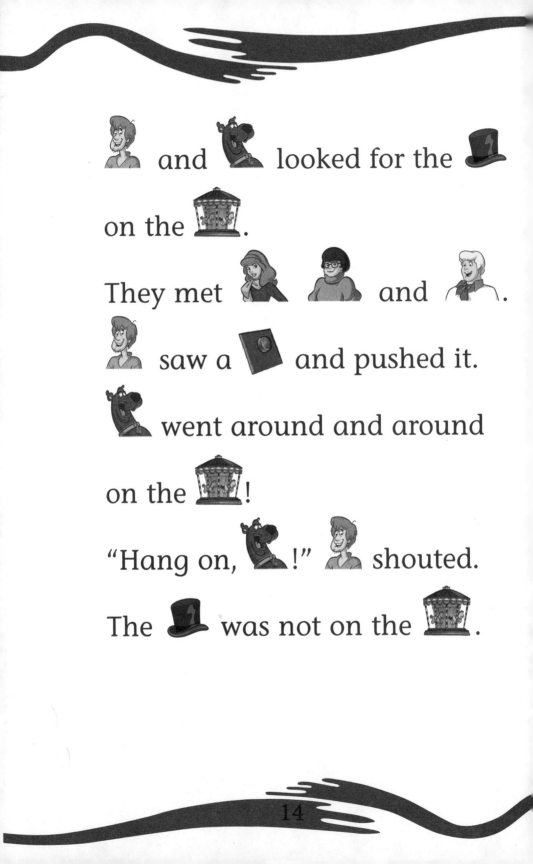

on the .

They met   and .

 saw a and pushed it.

 went around and around

on the !

"Hang on, !" shouted.

The was not on the .

"Jeepers!" 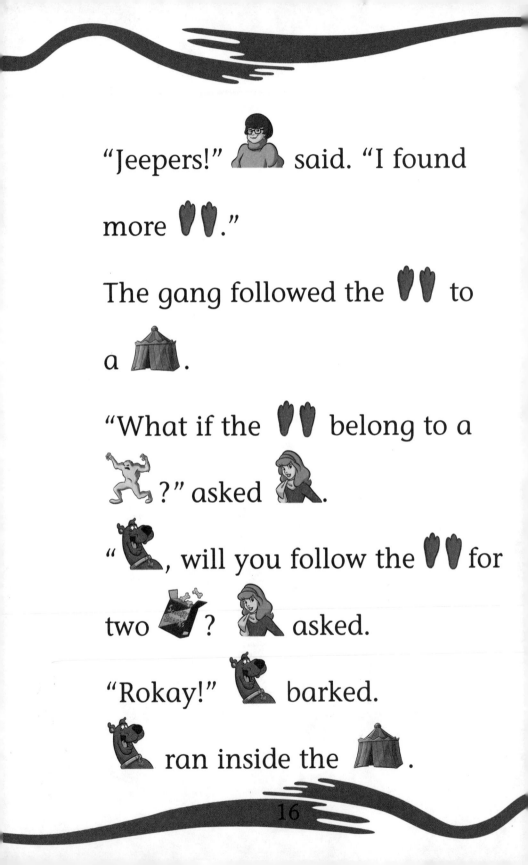 said. "I found

more 🐾."

The gang followed the 🐾 to

a ⛺.

"What if the 🐾 belong to a

🦍?" asked 👧.

"🐕, will you follow the 🐾 for

two 🦴? 👧 asked.

"Rokay!" 🐕 barked.

🐕 ran inside the ⛺.

A  was juggling some

inside the

A  sat on the 's shoulder.

The  was on the 's head!

"Jinkies!"  shouted. "The

has the !"

The  was surprised. The

dropped the  on his .

The  jumped off the .

The hopped over to .

"That made the we

saw!" said.

The ran inside the .

"There is my !" the

shouted. "And there is my !"

"I found the  inside this

🎪," the 🤡 said. "The 🐰 was

inside the 🎩. I used your 🎩

and your 🐰 in my show."

"That's great!" the 🎩 said. "My

🎩 and my 🐰 can be in both

shows."

"Scooby-Dooby Doo!" 🐕

barked.

Did you spot all the picture clues in this Scooby-Doo mystery?

Each picture clue is on a flash card. Ask a grown-up to cut out the flash cards. Then try reading the words on the back of the cards. The pictures will be your clue.

Reading is fun with Scooby-Doo!

tent	Scooby-Doo
balloons	monster
bowl	Scooby Snacks

magician	Shaggy
goldfish	peanuts
hat	clown

bunny	Velma
stuffed animals	popcorn
Fred	balls

footprints	Daphne
carousel	cotton candy
button	shoes